THE KINGDOM OF FANGS

MANASA SANDANABOINA

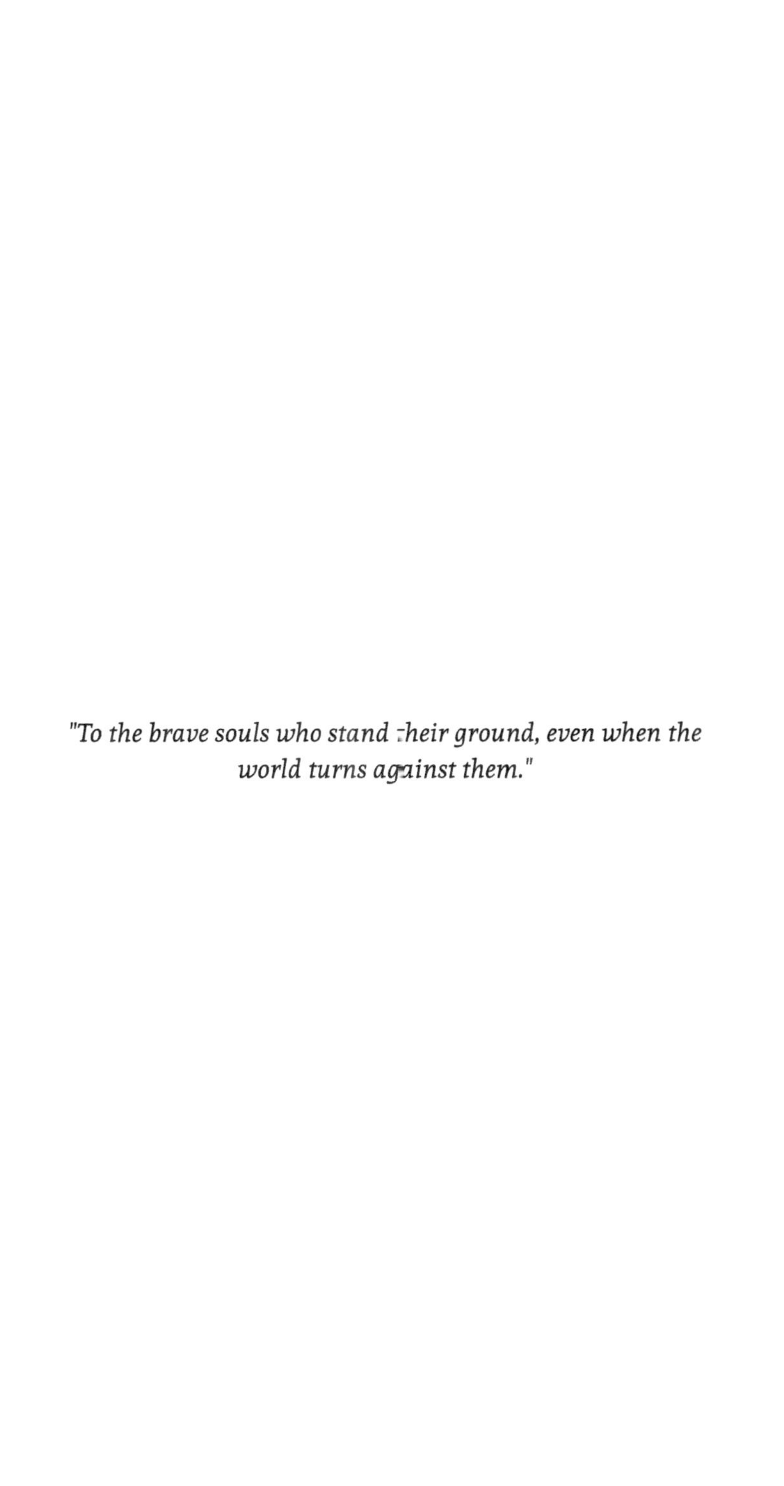

"To the brave souls who stand their ground, even when the world turns against them."

Contents

Foreword

In a world where stories of courage, loyalty, and survival are more needed than ever, Kingdom of Fangs stands as a vivid reminder of the battles we all face — both seen and unseen.

Manasa Sandanaboina's writing captures the pulse of bravery and hope, breathing life into characters that linger in the mind long after the last page is turned.

This book is not just a tale of war and loyalty; it's a tribute to the strength that lies within every soul fighting their own unseen battles.

It is my pleasure to introduce Kingdom of Fangs to you — a story born from passion, courage, and an unbreakable spirit.

Preface

Kingdom of Fangs was born from a deep love for stories that explore courage, loyalty, and the strength hidden within even the smallest of beings.

This book is my attempt to capture the spirit of survival and the quiet heroism that often goes unnoticed. Every character, every moment was shaped with the hope of inspiring those who might be facing battles of their own.

Writing this story was a journey of passion, imagination, and resilience, and I hope that as you turn each page, you find a part of yourself within this world.

Thank you for choosing to step into the Kingdom — where bravery wears many faces and hope never dies.

— Manasa Sandanaboina

Acknowledgements

Kingdom of Fangs is a product of countless hours of imagination, reflection, and perseverance.

I am deeply grateful to the unseen inspirations — the silent battles, the fleeting dreams, and the endless possibilities that gave life to this story.

To every reader who dares to dream beyond limits, and to every soul who believes in the power of resilience — this book is for you.

Thank you for being part of this journey.

— Manasa Sandanaboina

Prologue

Long before the first roar echoed through the valleys and before the first claw marked the stones, the Kingdom of Fangs was born in blood and silence.

A pact was forged — not by kings, but by the ancients who ruled before memory began. A pact that promised strength to the worthy and destruction to the weak.

But promises are fragile in a land where loyalty fades like mist and power hungers like a beast.

In the shadow of forgotten legends, a new era stirs. One where fangs will clash, crowns will fall, and a kingdom's fate will rest not on the sharpness of teeth — but on the strength of hearts willing to bleed for it.

The battle for the Kingdom of Fangs has begun.

1

The Law of the Pack's

There was a world untouched by humans—a world where paws, not hands, shaped kingdoms. Where the wind carried howls and the earth remembered pawprints, there stood a realm born of strength and loyalty.

This is **The Kingdom of Fangs**—a vast and ancient land ruled entirely by dogs.

Not pets, not strays, but wise and powerful beings who built a life of their own.

They were leaders, warriors, messengers, scholars, and guardians of the land.

This kingdom was built by paws.

A place where howls echo across the skies and every pawprint writes the path of destiny.

From the smallest pup to the mightiest Alpha, every dog has a role in keeping peace and balance.

They speak their own language.

They live by their own traditions.

And above all, they follow a sacred code passed down through generations—**The Laws of the Wild.**

The greatest of these laws is simple:

No dog shall kill another.

They believe in justice, not cruelty. In honour, not fear. Conflicts may rise—but they are settled with strength, strategy, and wisdom—not bloodshed.

High above the land, soaring through the clouds, fly the birds—ravens, eagles, and owls—

trusted messengers between packs. Though they do not rule, they are respected and vital, carrying secrets, warnings, and news across the skies.

The Kingdom of Fangs is divided into **five mighty packs**, each with its own strengths, lands, and way of life. Though different, they are all bound by one unshakable truth:

The Laws of the Wild protect them all.

1. The Pack of Valor:

Main Breeds: German Shepherd, Belgian Malinois, Indian Pariah, Mudhol Hound, Rajapalayam, Kombai.

Leader:*King Blaze – a strong and respected German Shepherd*

The Pack of Valor lives in the centre of the Kingdom of Fangs. Their land looks like a military city, built with stone walls, strong towers, and open training fields. Every dog here has a purpose—from young pups learning to fight, to old warriors training the next generation.

They live in proper houses made of stone and wood, built in straight lines like army camps. At the heart of the pack is the **Hall of Justice**, where King Blaze holds meetings and solves problems with the help of senior warriors.

This pack trains the best guards, trackers, and patrol teams. You can see dogs running drills, jumping through obstacles, or guarding the borders. They wake up early, follow strict rules, and believe in hard work, loyalty, and protection.

They are not just fighters—they are protectors of the entire kingdom. If any other pack is in danger, the Pack of

Valor is the first to arrive.

2. The Pack of Wisdom:

Main Breeds: Golden Retriever, Border Collie, Saluki, Shih Tzu, Afghan Hound, Maltese.

Leader:*Queen Elara – a graceful and wise Golden Retriever*

The Pack of Wisdom lives in a peaceful valley surrounded by rivers and trees. Their kingdom is calm and beautiful, filled with white stone temples, wide green gardens, and schools built under ancient trees. Birds often visit their land, sitting on rooftops and whispering messages from other packs.

The dogs here live in quiet houses made of polished stone and soft grass roofs. Inside, there are shelves of scrolls, old books, and drawings from the past. This pack runs the **Library of Echoes**, where every law, legend, and stories are stored. Pups grow up learning history, healing skills, and the Laws of the Wild.

Queen Elara walks among her people like a teacher, not a ruler. She guides with calm words and deep knowledge. The dogs of this pack are healers, scholars, and advisors to the other packs. When there is confusion or conflict, they bring clarity with their wisdom.

They believe knowledge is the strongest weapon—and peace is the greatest victory.

3. The Pack of Trade:

Main Breeds: Beagle, Pug, Dachshund, Corgi, Dalmatian, Cocker Spaniel, Chow-Chow, Yorkshire Terrier.

Leader:*Duke Winston – a clever and cheerful Beagle*

The Pack of Trade lives in the heart of the kingdom, where the roads from all five packs meet. Their land is always lively—colourful banners flying, sweet smells filling the air, and the sound of barking laughter echoing through the market streets.

Their kingdom is like a festival every day. Dogs live in cozy, bright houses with curved rooftops and hanging lights. The streets are lined with **food stalls, shops, craft centres, and news corners.** From golden biscuits to herbal remedies, everything is bought and sold here.

Duke Winston, the cheerful and clever Beagle, he watches over his kingdom from a tall tower or visits the market square on special days. When he appears, everyone gathers with joy. He wears a cape decorated with shiny coins and carries a small bag filled with scrolls and messages, showing his role as a wise and trusted leader.

Under his guidance, the **Pack of Trade** is strong and respected. They handle messages, trading goods, and sharing stories between all the packs. Young pups are trained to speak different languages, follow scents from far away, and tell powerful stories that can bring peace and friendship. Their messengers are quick, smart, and trusted by all.

This pack believes that connection builds unity, and trade brings peace.

4. The Pack of Blood Fang:

Main Breeds: Rottweiler, Doberman, Pit Bull, Kangal, Labrador.

Led by *King Kael*: *a fearless Rottweiler known for his unmatched strength and unwavering loyalty.*

Among all the packs, **the Pack of Blood Fang is the strongest**—not just in muscle, but in spirit and honour. Once feared for their aggression, these dogs have rewritten their legacy. They are no longer symbols of destruction, but guardians of power, protectors of borders, and enforcers of peace.

Their kingdom rises like a living monument to strength. **Not a fortress—but a citadel**, carved from dark stone and steel, standing firm on the edge of the kingdom's wild borders. Inside, massive training arenas, legendary battle shrines, and warrior halls echo with the disciplined rhythm of drills and ancient chants. Statues of fallen heroes line the roads, and every pup is raised knowing: strength is not for chaos—it is for protection.

They do not roam the land for glory. They wait. They train. They watch.

And **when a final decision must be made**—in times of war, threat, or betrayal—**it is Blood Fang that delivers the kingdom's justice.**

They are the final Défense, the last roar, and the unshakable wall between danger and peace.

5. The Pack of Sky Watchers:

Main Breeds: Husky, Akita, Shiba Inu, Bernese Mountain Dog, Samoyed, Pomeranian

Led by *Commander Nova*: *A majestic Siberian Husky with eyes like frozen stars and a heart full of silence and strength.*

High above the rest of the Kingdom of Fangs, where the snow never melts and the winds sing ancient songs, live the mysterious and noble **Pack of Sky Watchers**. Perched on icy cliffs and hidden peaks, their kingdom is a world of white serenity—**a realm sculpted from snow, stone, and sky**.

Their homes are carved into mountainsides, surrounded by icy forests and frozen lakes that reflect the stars. They live in harmony with the birds—especially the owls and eagles—who share their skies and serve as scouts and companions.

The Sky Watchers are **the eyes of the kingdom**. They read the weather, predict danger from the winds, and guard the highest borders from unseen threats. While other packs look forward, they look above. While others fight with paws, they protect with knowledge and foresight.

They speak little, observe much, and move like shadows across the snow. To outsiders, they seem distant. But in truth, **they are the silent guardians of balance**, warning the kingdom before storms, invasions, or unnatural shifts.

Commander Nova is said to speak to the winds themselves. When she howls, the mountains listen.

2

The Lone Dog Kaito

The sun rose gently over the Pack of Trade, casting golden rays onto the cobbled streets. The sweet smell of warm buns and spiced rolls drifted from *Muffin's Bakery*, a cozy little spot run by a chubby pug with flour on his nose and laughter in his voice.

Inside, *Kaito*, the scruffy mixed-breed with sharp eyes and a sharper tongue, was busy stacking trays while dodging Muffin's slow but steady tail-wags.

"Rolo!" Muffin barked from behind the counter, "Stop daydreaming and flip those croissants!"

Rolo, a long, lazy Dachshund with sleepy eyes and a permanently half-open mouth, sighed dramatically. "I would, Muffin... but she's late today."

"She?" Kaito raised a brow, knowing exactly where this was going.

Rolo sighed again, even louder this time. "*Rosie*, the Yorkshire Terrier with the long, shiny hair... she comes every morning for her sugar bun. And a smile. For *me*, obviously."

Kaito chuckled, flicking a breadcrumb at him. "Bro, she doesn't even know your name."

"She will," Rolo said dreamily. "One day, we'll run a bakery together. Me, her, and maybe a dozen little Yorkie-Dachshund pups."

Kaito snorted. "Yeah, and maybe her hair will stop growing too. It's longer than Muffin's shopping list."

"Hey, don't mock the hair," Rolo said, wagging his tail. "It flows like a waterfall."

"More like a mop that skipped the salon for five years," Kaito grinned.

Just then, the bell above the bakery door jingled.

Rolo sat up so fast he nearly knocked over the tray of buns.

There she was — *Rosie*, the petite Yorkshire Terrier with a sparkly bow, elegant paws, and the same graceful bounce in her step.

Rolo melted.

Kaito elbowed him. "Your waterfall just walked in."

As Rosie stepped up to the counter, Muffin greeted her with a cheerful, "The usual, Miss Rosie? One sugar bun with extra sparkle?"

Rosie giggled and nodded politely. "You always remember, Muffin."

Rolo stood frozen, his tail wagging nervously, eyes wide like he'd seen a goddess. "H-Hey Rosie... uh... nice weather today... I mean your hair looks like the weather—no, wait..."

"Kaito covered his face with a paw and muttered sarcastically, "Smooth, Romeo..."

Just as Rosie turned with her bun and a tiny thank-you, the bakery bell jingled again. This time, it was *Brock*, a stocky, no-nonsense Corgi with a wide chest, a short temper, and a deep grudge.

He stomped up to the counter and barked, "Still waiting for my meat rolls, Muffin. I ordered ten minutes ago."

Before Muffin could reply, Brock's sharp eyes darted to Rolo. "Let me guess. Lover-boy over here forgot again—too busy drooling over golden looks and dreaming about impossible fairy tales."

Rolo flinched, muttering, "I didn't forget. I was just—"

"You *always* forget *my* order." Brock snapped. "You think I don't see you? Watching her like a squirrel watch nuts in winter. She isn't yours, pal."

"Brock!" Muffin barked, stepping between them, "This is a peaceful bakery!"

But Kaito had already stepped in, placing a paw on Rolo's shoulder. "Alright, cool down. It's breakfast time, not bark-fight hour."

Brock narrowed his eyes at Rolo. "Just saying... not everyone enjoys the show."

Rolo looked down, ears drooping. Rosie, halfway out the door, gave one last look — not cold, not warm. Just unreadable.

A tense silence filled the bakery, broken only by the ticking of the old clock. Suddenly, the familiar chime of the village's emergency bell echoed through the streets—a sound reserved for the gravest of news.

Inside the bakery, conversations halted. Muffin's ears perked up, and he exchanged worried glances with Kaito and Rolo. The television mounted on the wall flickered, switching to the emergency broadcast channel.

A solemn voice filled the room:

"We bring grave news to all packs. King Kael of the Blood Fang and Commander Aeris of the Sky Watchers have been found dead in the Forest of Whispers."

Gasps erupted from the patrons. Muffin dropped a tray of pastries, the clatter echoing the shock in the room. Rolo's eyes widened, his mouth agape. Kaito's fur bristled, a deep growl rumbling from his throat.

The broadcast continued:

"Both leaders showed clear signs that they had been attacked." Effective immediately, all inter-pack borders are closed. No dog is to cross into another pack's territory without explicit council approval. This act has shattered the ancient law forbidding canine-on-canine violence."

A heavy silence settled over the bakery. The gravity of the situation was palpable, the air thick with disbelief and fear.

Outside Muffin's bakery, the evening air was thick with whispers. A group of dogs had gathered near a stall, their voices low but urgent.

"You saw the throat, right?" one elder dog barked, his eyes wide with disbelief. "It wasn't a dog's bite. It was… bigger."

"Then what was it?" another snapped, fur bristling. "A monster?"

"I'm telling you—this isn't just murder. This is a message."

The surrounding dogs froze, ears perked, eyes darting nervously. The weight of the words hung in the air, thickening the tension.

From the shadows, Kaito, the mixed-breed dog, listened intently. His keen ears caught every word, every tremor in the voices around him. He had always been observant, but tonight, the rumours felt different—darker, more dangerous.

A New King Rises

At the heart of the Pack of Blood Fang, drums echoed through the stone-carved valleys as news spread across the land:

General Drax, son of the fallen King Kael, had taken the throne.

Young, bold, and burning with fury, Drax stood before his grieving pack, eyes steady, voice like a battle cry wrapped in sorrow.

"My father was a king of honour. Aeris was the voice of peace.

I will not rest until their killer is found.

I swear by the blood of my line—we will uncover the darkness hiding in these shadows."

His speech was short, powerful, and shook the hearts of warriors across all kingdoms.

Within hours, giant posters covered pack walls—art of Kael's broken crown, Aeris's blue wings stained red, and bold letters screaming:

"WHO BROKE THE LAW? "

"WHO DARES TO WAKE THE OLD DARKNESS? "

News channels broadcast the images day and night. Magic-scroll posts floated mid-air. Even bakery wrappers were printed with bold warnings.

"One week of silence."

All six packs agreed—no travel, no meetings, no markets.

All territory gates were locked. No dog would move unless ordered.

Muffin, the ever-diligent Pug, sighed deeply.

"This is very scary news," he said, his voice tinged with concern. "As per the kingdom's orders, we need to close the bakery for a week. It's best we all take some rest."

Kaito nodded solemnly, his mind still racing with thoughts of King Kael's and Aeris's untimely deaths. The images from the news replayed in his mind, each one more haunting than the last.

Rolo, on the other hand, perked up with a grin.

"A whole week off? Finally, some time to relax!"

Muffin shot him a stern look.

"End of the day, I want everything cleared and put away neatly. You won't be coming in from tomorrow onwards, and not until next week."

As they began tidying up, a courier arrived with a letter bearing the Council's seal. Muffin opened it, his eyes scanning the contents quickly.

"The Council needs volunteers to deliver food and essential supplies to all the packs," he announced. "Given that the Trade Pack is the main provider for food-related services, it's our duty to help."

he turned to Kaito and Rolo.

"I've already agreed to send some bakery items—buns, dried meats, and herbal biscuits. But I need to know: will you two handle the delivery, or should I arrange for someone else?"

Before Kaito could respond, Rolo waved his paw dismissively.

"No way, Muffin. I just got my week off!"

Muffin raised an eyebrow.

"They'll compensate you for your time. It's just a two-days task, and you'll be back by the third day."

Upon hearing that the delivery was to the Blood Fang Pack, Kaito's ears perked up.

"Blood Fang Pack? I'll do it," he said firmly. "Rolo is coming with me."

Rolo's eyes widened.

"Wait, what? Why me?"

Kaito smirked.

"Because you owe me for covering your shifts last month. Plus, think of it as an adventure."

Muffin chuckled, jotting down their names on the delivery roster.

"Alright then. Kaito and Rolo, official couriers for the Trade Pack. Stay safe out there."

As the two friends prepared for their journey, the weight of their mission settled upon them. The road ahead was uncertain, but their resolve was firm.

Rolo sat silently; his usual jovial demeanour replaced with a sullen expression.

"Rolo, why are you so upset? It's just two days. I wouldn't go without you," Kaito said, trying to lighten the mood.

Rolo remained silent for a moment before responding, his voice tinged with frustration.

"Why, bro? Why are you doing this? Is it for the money?"

Kaito shook his head. "No, Rolo. This isn't about money. It's about my family."

Rolo's eyes widened in surprise. "What family? You're a street dog, right? You told me you were born in a pizza box, with leftover onions as pillows."

Kaito chuckled softly. "That's what I told you, but the truth is, I have a family. They wanted me to study and follow a path I didn't choose, so I ran away."

"Oh, stop it, Kaito. Your drama is too much," Rolo replied, rolling his eyes.

"No, Rolo, this is true. I need your help," Kaito said earnestly.

"But how will you meet your family? Do you know where they live?" Rolo asked, scepticism evident in his voice.

"I don't know exactly, but I believe they're in the Blood Fang Pack. Come with me, and I'll explain everything," Kaito pleaded.

Rolo hesitated, his mind racing with thoughts. "You're planning my murder, aren't you? I want to marry Rosie and have a bunch of children."

"Trust me, Rolo. Nothing will happen to you," Kaito assured him.

Crossing into Blood Fang Territory

Early the next morning, Kaito and Rolo prepared for their journey. They obtained the necessary approval letter from Dalmatian, the council representative, and loaded their food truck with bakery items.

As they approached the border, a large sign loomed ahead:

You are entering Blood Fang Territory – No Entry without Royal Seal

At the checkpoint, they were met by vigilant guards from the Pack Valor—German Shepherds and Belgian Malinois, known for their intelligence and agility.

Kaito presented the approval letter to the guards, who scrutinized it carefully before granting them passage.

As they entered the Blood Fang territory, the atmosphere grew tense. The once-familiar landscape now felt foreign and unwelcoming.

They arrived at the Blood Fang Pack territory late in the evening. The pit bull guard at the Warehouse gate looked at them sternly. "You're late. No deliveries accepted at night.

"Sorry, got held up," Kaito replied, trying to sound casual.

"No deliveries at night. Rest here. Deliver in the morning. Don't wander."

He handed them a room key and turned away.

Inside the room, Kaito spread out a map on the table.

"What's your plan now?" Rolo asked, raising an eyebrow. "Please, no heroics. One wrong move, and we're dog biscuits."

Kaito smiled reassuringly. "Just reviewing the map. Nothing more."

As Rolo drifted into a restless sleep, Kaito quietly prepared to leave.

Grabbing a torchlight and wearing a mask, he was determined to visit the forest where King Kael and Aeris were killed.

Just as he was about to step out, Rolo stirred. "Wait, where are you going?"

"Sorry, Rolo. I want to see my family."

"This isn't correct, and it's not the right time."

"Please, Rolo. I need to do this."

After some hesitation, Rolo sighed. "Fine, but be careful."

Kaito set off towards the forest, torchlight in hand. The forest was near their stay. Moving cautiously, the torchlight cast eerie shadows.

Kaito slipped away through the deeper woods, paws silent, breath steady.

The place where **King Kael** and **Aeris** died wasn't marked, but he remembered the direction from the patrols and the scent in the air—burnt bark, disturbed earth, fear.

And blood.

The clearing was silent, covered with fallen leaves, but Kaito's nose twitched.

He sniffed the edges, pacing in circles.

Then he saw it.

A small piece of **cloth**—torn, barely noticeable—stuck under a root.

It had a faint mark...a strange black paw print that didn't belong to any known pack. It wasn't royal. It wasn't trade.

"Someone outside was here," Kaito whispered.

A chill went through his fur.

Back at the room, Rolo was wide awake, pacing nervously. "If anyone comes, I'll just pretend to be asleep. But what if they check? Maybe I should hide under the bed...

No, that's too obvious."

When Kaito returned, red cloth in hand, Rolo exclaimed, "Finally! I thought they got you. Did you meet your family?"

Kaito sat beside him quietly.

"No, there's no home. It's okay; we'll search later. I'm with you."

They hugged, and in his heart, Kaito whispered a silent apology for the earlier lie. The next morning, they delivered the food to the store and started their journey back to the Trade Pack.

Still four days remained until the bakery would reopen. Kaito kept the red cloth hidden in his bag, his mind swirling with questions. The Trade Pack was unusually silent, a stillness that Kaito had never experienced before. He pondered, "Who are the enemies? Why was this done so cruelly? Whose paw print is this?" The symbol on the cloth offered no answers, only more mysteries.

Meanwhile, Rolo was enjoying his time off, lounging in their room. "Finally, some free time," he said, stretching out.

One day, a Chow Chow, an old and lazy dog, came to their home seeking help. Rolo, not wanting to be disturbed, said, "I'm busy, I won't come."

But Kaito responded, "I'll come, uncle." The old dog explained, "I'm too old; I can't lift things. My son and his family are stuck in the Wisdom Pack. They were working there and will return after four days."

Kaito nodded, "I understand. I'm also getting bored."

As they worked together, Kaito asked, "What do you think about the incident with the king? Who could have done such a thing?"

The Chow Chow looked around cautiously before speaking, "This is a symbol of our entire kingdom collapsing soon. Our law states that no dog kills another dog. In my entire career, I've never seen such a thing. Dogs die naturally, not by the paws of others."

Kaito was shocked. "Wait, are you saying this has happened before?"

The old dog nodded solemnly. "When I was a pup, my grandfather told me stories of cruel monsters that killed innocent dogs. They disappeared as suddenly as they appeared. I don't know who they were, but they left a mark."

Kaito's curiosity was piqued. "I want to know the history now. I don't read much, but maybe there's something out there."

The Chow Chow thought for a moment. "My son mentioned that in the Wisdom Pack, there's an old Sentinel—a Labrador who lectures on history at the school. He has some ancient history books. Maybe you'll find the answers you're looking for there.'

After his conversation with the Chow Chow, Kaito felt a renewed sense of purpose. He thought, "Once I visit the Wisdom Pack, I might finally get some answers." He waited patiently for the four days to pass.

When the four days were over, news channels announced, "All work is resuming as normal. However, to cross the border of any pack, you need proper permission."

Kaito was pleased with this news. He thought, "This is my chance to visit the Wisdom Pack and seek the knowledge I've been yearning for."

A Lie to Protect a brother

That night, while Rolo was asleep, Kaito stepped outside and looked at the stars.

"I'm sorry, Rolo," he whispered. "You're like a brother to me... That's why I can't let you get involved."

He had decided.

He was going to **find out who killed King Kael** and the other husky general, even if it meant walking into danger alone.

The Next Morning

At the bakery, Muffin the pug was preparing the morning dough when Kaito walked in.

"Sir," Kaito said quietly, "I need a month off."

Muffin blinked. "What for?"

Kaito hesitated, then said,

"I want to study... maybe history. I want to find where I come from."

Muffin stared for a few seconds, then gave a small nod.

"Come back soon."

Rolo's Tears

As Kaito packed, Rolo came running. "Bro! You're leaving? What happened?"

Kaito smiled. "I just want to learn something, that's all."

Rolo's eyes filled with tears. "You idiot... We've been together since pups! You're really going?"

Kaito knelt beside Rolo and placed a gentle paw on his shoulder.

"Take care of yourself, alright? Stay with Muffin and help out at the bakery.

And Rolo... don't forget where we came from."

Rolo looked down. Kaito continued, his voice softer,

"We were just a couple of street dogs—no home, no hope.

Muffin gave us more than shelter. He gave us a second chance.

Respect that. Hold it close."

Kaito glanced at the warm bakery behind them.

"He gave us space, gave us jobs.

Now it's our turn to protect what he built.

Promise me you'll stay strong, and keep that oven burning."

Rolo wiped his nose with a paw, blinking back tears. "You better come back soon."

Kaito nodded, fighting back emotion. "Take care of the bakery for me. And don't burn the bread this time."

They laughed again, but deep down, Kaito knew... this wasn't just a trip.

They hugged.

Kaito was doing this alone... to protect everyone he loved.

The Journey Begins

He took a dusty bus heading toward the mysterious and quiet region known as **The Pack of Wisdom**, home to ancient libraries, monks, and scholars.

Each bus stop, each road bump—Kaito's mind was focused.

"I saw something at that forest. A clue. A pawprint. This was not a wild attack... It was murder."

The cloth in his paw still held a faint scent... and Kaito was following it.

Along the way, Kaito sat next to a **Rudra** (Mudhol Hound) who worked as a patrol dog.

"You look too young to head toward Wisdom lands," Rudra said.

Kaito gave a slight grin. "I'm just chasing a story."

They talked for a while. The Rudra shared a few cases about lost dogs, missing leaders, and threats kept from public.

"Not everything is shown on the news," he said. "Some deaths are made to look like accidents. But they're not."

That one sentence echoed in Kaito's head.

3
Chasing Shadows

Arriving at Wisdom's Border

The dry wind blew gently as Kaito stood at the border of **The Pack of Wisdom.** The tall gates, carved with symbols of ancient dogs and battles, felt heavy with silence.

Two calm yet sharp-eyed **German Shepherds** and one athletic **Kombai** approached.

"Purpose of visit?" the elder German Shepherd asked.

Kaito cleared his throat, trying to appear calm. "I'm here to attend a one-month course on ancient dog history. I've heard there's a professor here who's an expert on old records and forgotten bloodlines."

The guards exchanged a look. One sniffed him lightly.

The Kombai, with a stern expression, said, "Do you have a permission letter from the Wisdom Pack Council?"

Kaito nodded, reaching into his bag. "Yes, I applied online and received permission to enter the Wisdom Pack and learn the history." He handed over the letter.

The Afghan Hound, Laila, stepped forward gracefully, her eyes scanning the letter. "This is from Queen Elara's office. Everything seems in order."

The elder German Shepherd returned the letter to Kaito. "Welcome to the Pack of Wisdom. Follow the path straight ahead to reach the main hall. Someone will guide you from there."

Kaito bowed slightly. "Thank you."

As he walked through the gates, he felt a mix of anticipation and curiosity. The journey to uncover the mysteries of the past had just begun.

The Streets of Silence

Kaito walked through the quiet stone streets. Here, dogs didn't bark. They whispered. No chasing, no noise. Every dog he passed either read scrolls or carried herbs.

He made his way toward the small **Wisdom School**, where puppies sat in neat rows under trees, studying from bone-shaped slates.

A sharp-looking **Border Collie**, wearing tiny round glasses and a neck bell, was barking facts about ancient leaders.

"What's the law of respect?"
"No bark shall be raised unless it brings truth!" the puppies shouted in unison.

Kaito waited politely. When the class ended, he walked up to the teacher and asked, "Sir, I'm looking for Professor Sentinel. I heard he teaches here sometimes?"

The Border Collie adjusted his glasses.

"Sentinel? Oh... He's too old now. He just visits when he's bored. You won't find him here today. Go see Headmaster Swift—he knows everything."

Inside the Wisdom Hall

The main hall of the school was peaceful. Books were stacked floor to ceiling. A gentle instrumental song played from a wind chime.

Kaito stepped inside, his claws tapping softly against the smooth tiles.

At the centre, reading a book so fast the pages blurred, sat **Headmaster Swift**—a slim, aged **Saluki** with flowing white fur and incredible speed-reading ability.

Without looking up, he said,

"You're not from around here."

"No sir. I came for learning... and for guidance."

Headmaster Swift looked up slowly. "You don't smell like a student."

Kaito's heart skipped. Was he caught?

"I'm curious," he said, hiding his thoughts. "I've heard stories of Sentinel. Is he still alive?"

Swift blinked. "Barely. But his nose still works."

He pulled out a small bone-scroll and scribbled an address.

"Go to the edge of Misty Lake. He stays in a hut shaped like a curled leaf. Don't expect much. He talks more to clouds than to dogs now."

Kaito nodded and whispered, "Thank you."

The journey to Misty Lake was quiet, almost magical. Birds flew in perfect patterns. An old **Shih Tzu librarian** helped Kaito with directions halfway through.

After crossing small stone bridges and stepping over roots, Kaito reached the hut—a worn, twisted little place leaning near the lake, covered in moss.

He stepped inside.

The room was silent, except for the soft wheeze of old lungs.

Kaito sat awkwardly, unsure if the professor was awake or dreaming.

Then, the old Labrador's gravelly voice broke the silence.

"Why are you really here?"

Kaito hesitated. "I told you, sir. I came to learn history."

Professor Sentinel turned slowly, his tired eyes sharpening like claws.

"What history?" he asked, voice firmer now.

Kaito swallowed. "The packs. Their stories. Their beginnings."

For a moment, there was silence. Then the old dog growled faintly.

"Which pack are you from?"

"Trade Pack," Kaito replied.

"Then go back. Do your trading. Sell bread. Count coins. Why waste time chasing dead tales?"

Kaito looked down. His heart sank. He had come so far, only to be rejected.

"I... I just want to know the truth."

Sentinel turned his back, clearly done with the conversation.

Kaito stood up slowly. As he reached for his bag, a piece of cloth slipped out and floated to the ground like a falling leaf.

The paw-printed cloth.

Sentinel turned his head sharply.

"Wait."

He sniffed the air.

"That cloth... where did you get that?"

He closed the door with a sudden bang, locking it.

"Who are you?" he demanded, stepping closer. "Where did you find this?"

Kaito's throat dried. But he spoke calmly.

"At the scene where the Blood Pack King was murdered. I found it near a blood trail. No one else noticed it."

The old dog trembled. His paws pressed against the cloth.

"This... This doesn't belong in that territory," he whispered.

He looked up, his voice grave. "What do you want to do with this information, pup?"

Kaito's eyes didn't waver.

"I want to know who broke the sacred rules. Who ended peace between packs. Everyone says something different. Some say it was an inside job. Others say it was rogues. But I want the *real* truth."

The old dog stared at him, his breathing shallow.

"If you take this road... it's no trail walk. You'll lose everything. This path takes your sleep, your peace... and maybe your life. Go back to your bakery, pup. Let the elders deal with this."

Kaito stepped forward, firm and still.

"Sir, I don't have a family to lose. I don't have a home to protect. I have nothing... except a reason to go on."

His voice cracked—but he didn't stop.

"If I die finding the truth, at least I'll be useful once in this life."

Sentinel looked away, eyes wet, lips trembling.

"You remind me of someone... foolish and brave."

Kaito gently pushed the cloth toward him.

"If anything happens to me, tell Muffin and Rolo that I came back early. That I... couldn't finish what I started."

Silence again.

The old Labrador took a deep breath, as if inhaling Kaito's courage.

Then he spoke:

"Alright, pup. If you're that determined... I'll show you where the shadows begin."

The old Labrador, **Sentinel**, lit a small lantern and led Kaito down the dark, creaky stairs beneath the house.

The air grew colder, and the scent of old paper, Mold, and ancient ink filled Kaito's nose.

A heavy wooden door opened with a groan. Inside lay a hidden **library** untouched by time.

Dust blanketed rows of ancient books.

"This place is older than any pack still standing," Sentinel whispered. "Not even the Pack of Wisdom dares to open these books."

Kaito's eyes widened, stepping carefully between the shelves as if scared to disturb the silence of forgotten history.

Sentinel's paw traced along the cracked spines until it stopped on one thick, blackened book with claw marks on the cover.

He blew the dust off.

"The True Packs of the Beginning."

He placed it on a table, opened it with trembling paws, and flipped through yellowed pages until he stopped.

The faded ink revealed a **sixth emblem**.

A jagged skull over a pile of bones. The symbol sent chills down Kaito's spine.

"I thought there were only five packs," Kaito whispered.

Sentinel shook his head.

"That's what the world is told. But before our history was sealed in peace, there was one more pack... ***The Bone Eaters***."

Kaito's ears perked up.

"Bone Eaters...?"

"Yes," Sentinel said gravely. "A pack so dangerous... even their name was erased from stories. They were monsters in dog's skin. They fed on the remains of war, and not just bones... but flesh."

Kaito froze. "What?!"

Sentinel turned the page. A terrifying sketch of Bone Eater warriors, eyes glowing, jaws dripping blood.

"Their king... **Varkor**, the Bone-Crowned Tyrant. No mercy. No law. Only hunger."

Kaito leaned in, heart racing.

"What happened to them?"

"The five original packs—**Wisdom**, **Trade**, **Valor**, **Sky Watchers**, and **Blood Fang**—joined together in one final war. Thousands died. Cities turned to ash. But together, they destroyed the Bone Eaters' kingdom. Buried it in silence. And made one final rule..."

He pointed to a page with a law carved in red ink:

"No dog shall ever take the life of another. For we paid for peace with our blood."

Kaito stood silent, every hair on his body standing on edge.

"But..." Sentinel said slowly, pulling out the red cloth from the table, "this cloth... it bears the **symbol** of the Bone Eaters. The old pawprint. The blood-stained mark."

Kaito gasped. "You mean... they're alive?"

Sentinel's voice dropped into a whisper.

"That's the rumour. That Varkor's bloodline survived. And now, they're rising again... in shadows."

Kaito's mind spun.

"We must tell the police! They'll—"

"No," Sentinel growled, slamming the book shut. "They won't believe you. They'll say *you* killed the king. They'll say you made up stories. They'll arrest you. And your friends, your bakery, even your pack—will be destroyed in fear."

Kaito backed away.

"But... what do we do?"

Sentinel gave a tired chuckle, almost mocking, yet filled with sorrow.

"And what will you do if you find them, pup? What will one street dog do against a forgotten nightmare?"

Kaito stood up and looked directly at him.

"I'll dig out their roots. I'll find where they're hiding, gather proof, and give it to the police... to all pack leaders. I'll make them see the truth. I'll shake the silence."

He took a breath, then added:

"If this darkness is rising again... maybe it's time to break our sacred rule. If it comes to protecting the innocent, to saving our packs..."

He looked up with eyes filled with fire.

"Then yes... if it's death or destruction—**we must learn to kill again.**"

Sentinel was stunned.

The quiet room felt heavier, like the air itself was listening.

"Those are dangerous words Kaito," Sentinel said. "Once a pack forgets mercy, we return to the bones we buried. But maybe... maybe you're right. Maybe we need a dog who doesn't carry royal blood... but carries **courage.**"

Kaito asked quietly, "Do you know where they're living now?"

Sentinel sat down slowly, his paws trembling.

"The truth is... after the Bone Eaters were destroyed, the **Blood Fang Pack** rose from their ashes. They took control of the central kingdom. They erased the old name and replaced it with power."

"Some believe... *the Bone Eaters never truly died.* That a few escaped. Fled to the forests beyond the borders, deep in places where no pack dares to patrol."

"If they're alive... they're hiding. Quiet. Breeding in silence. Training their young in the old ways."

Kaito narrowed his eyes.

"Then we find the forest."

"Even if you do… they'll smell you before you get close. Bone Eaters aren't just dangerous… they're **ancient. Born of war. Raised in shadows.** They don't fear death—they *devour it.*"

"But," Sentinel whispered, leaning forward, "there's something else."

Kaito waited.

"There's one old whisper… that the Bone Eaters left behind a trail. Clues. Symbols. Their kind can't resist marking their territory. If you find a **three-clawed slash with a skull**, you're close."

Kaito nodded. "Then that's where I'll start."

Sentinel paused.

"Be careful, Kaito. You're not hunting a story… you're walking into one. And stories like these? They *eat their heroes.*"

A Stranger's Kindness:

The sky was painted in dull Gray, as if the heavens, too, were unsure about what came next.

Kaito sat on an old wooden bench near the edge of the **Forestview Market**. His paws were sore, his eyes tired from sleepless nights. His mind echoed Sentinel's words— "They eat their heroes."

"*Where do I start…?*" Kaito whispered to himself, staring at the ground.

Suddenly, a calm but energetic voice broke his thoughts.

"Hey bro, are you okay? You look like you haven't eaten or slept in days."

Kaito looked to his right. A strong-built **Boxador** (Boxer + Labrador mix) with warm eyes and a bright red collar was sitting beside him, wagging his tail. He had a kind smile that made him look more like a big brother than a stranger.

"Hi… I'm from Trade Pack. My name's Kaito," he said, hesitantly.

The dog gave a friendly nod.

"Nice to meet you, Kaito. I'm **Bruno**-also from Trade Pack, working in Wisdom pack. Just came back from delivery. You seriously look exhausted, bro."

He examined Kaito a bit.

"Are you… crossbreed?" he asked, blinking curiously.

Kaito looked away, a bit stunned.

"I-I don't know. I never met my parents. I grew up on the streets…"

Bruno instantly looked guilty and softened his voice.

"Ah no no, bro! Don't take it the wrong way—I didn't mean any offense. Most of us here are mixed breeds. I was just curious, that's all."

He paused, then added gently:

"I'm really sorry to hear that."

Bruno stood up and stretched

"You know what? You can't sleep on benches like this. Come home with me. My wife makes amazing stew. You'll love it."

Kaito blinked, unsure.

"Really? I mean… it's okay, I don't want to trouble—"

"No bro, come on. You need some rest. That's what a real pack means—even strangers help each other."

Kaito gave a small smile.

Bruno had a simple but cozy scooter-like wooden cart with paw-steered wheels. He helped Kaito into it and drove toward the northern side of the wisdom Pack territory.

After 20 minutes of scenic travel through narrow mud paths, chirping birds, and market stalls, they reached a sweet little wooden house nestled under a mango tree. Outside the door, a nameplate carved in bone wood read:

"The Happy Bark Family"
Waiting at the door were:

- **Luna**, Bruno's wife – a golden **Cocker Spaniel** with gentle eyes and a warm voice.
- **Bolt**, their eldest – a 7-month-old energetic son.
- **Snowy**, their daughter – a fluffy 4-month-old, with one floppy ear.

"Oh! You brought a guest?" Luna asked, wiping her paws on a mat.

"Yeah, he's Kaito. From Trade Pack. Long day. Let's give him a night to breathe," Bruno replied.

They all greeted Kaito with wagging tails. Snowy even brought him her favourite toy ball and placed it by his paws shyly.

Luna served warm **chicken-veg stew** with soft bread bones. The aroma filled the room, and Kaito's stomach rumbled. It had been days since he'd eaten a proper meal.

"So, what brings you to wisdom pack?" Bruno asked during dinner.

Kaito thought for a second, then gave a gentle smile.

"Just a small one-month course. History topic. Just wanted to meet a professor."

"Ahh! You're the smart kind, huh?" Bruno chuckled. "Wish I had studied. I just run deliveries and help build dog houses."

After dinner, they all curled up under warm leaf blankets. Kaito had a small bed in the corner beside the fireplace. It had a pillow shaped like a bone.

Luna whispered, "Sleep well, dear. You're safe tonight."

As everyone fell asleep, Kaito lay awake for a moment, staring at the wooden ceiling.

"Safe for now..." he thought. *"But tomorrow, the real journey continues."*

The early sunlight peeked through the trees of the **Wisdom Pack's Forest edge**, casting a golden hue across the ground. Birds chirped, and the smell of wet grass filled the air.

Kaito woke up to the soft nudge of Bruno's nose.

"Good morning, Kaito! Slept peacefully?" Bruno asked, wagging his tail.

Kaito stretched and gave a rare, calm smile.

"Yes, Bruno. Best sleep I've had in days... Thank you."

Bruno grinned.

"That's what we're here for bro! But hey, I've got an urgent delivery today—way out near the river border. I might not be back tonight."

Kaito blinked.

"Oh! Okay... I'll find a way to head out then."

But Bruno quickly raised a paw.

"No, no—don't rush. This part of the forest isn't exactly crowded. Very few dogs live nearby. It gets quiet after sunset. I'll feel better if you stay here with Luna and the pups. Just tonight. Tomorrow morning, I'll return and drop you wherever you want."

Kaito looked into Bruno's eyes—there was genuine concern there.

He thought of how Bruno welcomed him, fed him, gave him a bed without knowing anything about his past. Even though his mind was restless with thoughts of the **Bone Eaters**, his heart felt something warm he hadn't felt in years—**trust.**

"Alright, I'll stay. No need to request, Bruno. Go happily," Kaito replied. "I'll take care of your family. I owe you that much."

Bruno's tail thumped with joy.

"You're a good dog, Kaito. I knew it the moment I saw you on that bench."

He gave Kaito a friendly nudge, said goodbye to Luna and the pups, and rolled off on his delivery cart, disappearing down the dusty trail.

That day, Kaito played with Bolt and Snowy, helped Luna clean up the backyard, and even fixed a wobbly wooden fence near the edge of the garden. But his thoughts kept drifting back to what Sentinel had said:

"Bone Eaters... if they're back, no one is safe."

As the evening crept in, the forest around the house turned quiet—almost too quiet.

Luna lit a small lamp near the door and placed a bone whistle beside Kaito.

"If you hear or see anything strange, blow this. The elders will hear and come."

Kaito nodded.

"Thank you, Luna."

That night, as the pups slept and Luna dozed off in her rocking chair, Kaito sat near the window, eyes scanning the forest.

"Where are you hiding, Bone Eaters..." he whispered.

Just then... a soft **rustling** sound echoed from the trees.

Kaito's ears perked up.

A shadow... fast. Four-legged. But gone in a blink.

He didn't blow the whistle. Not yet.

He needed to be sure.

"Tomorrow, when Bruno returns... I'll tell him. And then... maybe I'll follow that shadow."

Kaito's journey had just taken a turn.

The warm sunlight slowly broke through the tree leaves as morning arrived. Birds chirped, and the fresh scent of dew filled the forest.

Bruno returned, pulling his small wooden cart, his face full of energy and a smile.

"Good morning, Kaito! I'm back early today."

Kaito stood waiting near the fence and looked serious.

"Bruno... last night, I saw something. A shadow, fast. It wasn't any normal forest dog."

Bruno paused. His face tightened for a moment, then he laughed casually.

"Haha... bro, it happens here. Might be a loner dog. Forest plays tricks in the dark."

But deep inside, Bruno felt something wasn't right. He looked back toward the forest, his tail slightly stiff, eyes scanning the trees.

"Still... I'd say don't go too deep in there. Some parts haven't been visited in years. It's not safe."

Kaito nodded, but his mind was already made up.

He turned toward Luna, who had just come out holding a small cloth bundle.

"Kaito, if you really want to go... take this. I packed some food—bones, dry fish, and berries. This knife might help if you feel danger. And here's the lamp. It'll give you light for the whole night."

"Thank you, Luna. I'll be careful," Kaito said softly.

Luna looked worried but trusted him. Bruno stood quietly, unsure whether to stop Kaito or let him go.

"Bruno, thank you for everything. Tell your pups I'll come back and play again soon," Kaito said, forcing a smile.

"Stay safe, brother. Come back... in one piece," Bruno replied, giving him a small paw shake.

The Forest's Silence

Kaito stepped into the forest alone. His legs pushed through thick grass, dried leaves crackled beneath his paws, and old trees towered above like silent guards. Time passed—no tracks, no sound, just endless green.

Hours later, just before nightfall, Kaito reached the riverbank.

The water was calm, the air cooler, and stars had just begun to show.

"I'll rest here tonight. Start again tomorrow morning," he whispered.

He placed the bundle Luna gave him on the soft ground.

He chewed the dry fish, drank from the river, and slowly lit the small lamp. Its soft orange light made the shadows around him look less scary.

Then, curling up beside a tree trunk, Kaito laid his head down, his paw still resting near the knife.

"Bone Eaters... where are you?" he whispered to the wind.

The forest answered with silence.

The lamp flickered softly as Kaito closed his eyes.

Morning sunlight kissed the surface of the river as birds flew low across the water. The air was cool, and the forest felt calmer than before.

Kaito slowly opened his eyes, stretched his paws, and looked around.

"Nothing happened last night... maybe I was wrong," he murmured to himself.

He stood up, feeling fresher and more clear-headed. He ate the leftover berries and bones Luna had packed.

"I searched the whole area. No clues. No paw prints. Nothing strange. Maybe I'm in the wrong place."

Kaito walked along the river, watching the water flow steadily.

"Should I go back? Or... go forward?"

He looked across the river. The other side was wild, untouched—dense forest with thick vines and tall, dark trees.

But the river was wide. Swimming across with his bag and knife would be too risky.

"I can't swim with this weight. I need to build something... something to help me cross."

The Boat Plan

Kaito made his decision.

He gathered strong sticks, dry logs, and tree bark. He cut down small straight trees using the knife Luna gave him.

It wasn't easy.

His paws were scratched, and his body ached. He tied the logs using old vines he found wrapped around the rocks.

For hours, he worked—pulling, cutting, dragging.

Slowly, the shape of a small raft-like boat began to form.

He used flat bark pieces as the base, supported by logs tied tight. He found a long stick to use as a paddle.

By sunset, the boat was ready. It wasn't perfect, but it could float.

Kaito collapsed beside it, breathing heavily, fur messy with sweat and dirt.

"That's enough for today... I'll cross tomorrow morning."

His stomach growled.

As he walked to the river's edge to drink water, he spotted small fish swimming near the rocks.

He quickly used the stick and his knife to catch a few.

He gathered dry twigs and set a small fire using a spark from the lamp and rubbed rocks. Carefully, he grilled the fish over the flames, the smell filling the air.

Sitting quietly beside the fire, with the river flowing and the forest singing softly in the background, Kaito finally smiled a little.

"Thanks, Luna... this food is perfect."

After eating, he checked the boat one last time, pulled it near a rock to keep it from drifting, and then curled up beside the fire.

The stars above were brighter than ever.

"Tomorrow... I'll go beyond."

Kaito was deep in sleep, the warmth of the fire slowly dying beside him.

Suddenly... **crack.**

A sound came from the forest.

Kaito's ears perked up.

He sat up quickly, eyes scanning the darkness. The trees stood silent, but something moved—**a shadow.**

"That same shadow again..." he whispered, his heart racing.

Without wasting a moment, he grabbed his knife and lamp and followed.

The shadow was fast, weaving between trees and disappearing into the darkness.

Kaito tried to keep up—but just like before—he **lost it.**

Breathing heavily, Kaito leaned against a tree. Then he heard something strange.

Vrrrrrrr....

A soft vehicle sound. Quiet. Hidden. But it was nearby.

Kaito crouched low and followed the sound.

Through the bushes, near the riverbank, he saw it—**a small vehicle** parked behind the trees.

It looked **just like Bruno's.**

"But many dogs have this model... can't be sure."

He stayed low and crept forward.

Suddenly, he noticed **a boat** coming down the river.

He hid behind a large tree, barely peeking out.

The boat stopped at the shore.

Three figures got down—faces hidden behind dark masks. Their fur couldn't be seen, only black suits, and strange symbols on their arms. They carried sacks and boxes.

And then...

Bruno.

Kaito's eyes widened.

Bruno stepped forward from the trees and handed something to the masked dogs—**a small packet wrapped in red cloth.**

The lamp's light flickered on Bruno's face, and for a second... **he looked sad**.

Kaito's heart pounded. He couldn't believe what he was seeing.

"Is Bruno helping them...? Why?"

After the masked dogs got on the boat and left, Kaito slowly came out from the trees to follow Bruno.

But before Kaito could take a step—**a strong paw pulled him back hard.**

"Don't! Are you mad?" Bruno whispered harshly, dragging him into the shadows.

Bruno's eyes were wide with fear.

"If they see you, you're finished! No one can know I'm helping you. They'll kill you... they'll kill my whole family."

Bruno took Kaito back home, silent the entire walk. Inside, they sat near the fireplace.

Kaito couldn't hold it anymore.

"Bruno... what was that shadow? Who were those masked dogs?"

Bruno sighed heavily. "Even I don't know exactly who they are. But I can tell... they're not ordinary dogs. They're part of *this land*, but different. Dangerous. Trained."

Kaito leaned in. "You've seen them before?"

"No... not their faces. Never. They're always masked. But from their build, the way they move, their strength... they're not just some forest scavengers. They're trained fighters. Maybe even from the past."

Kaito's eyes widened. "Then... you're helping them?"

Bruno looked down.

"At first... I didn't know. I thought they were just a secret trading group. They never spoke a word. Every morning, they left a note in front of my garden. A simple paper, listing what they needed—rations, medicine, cloaks, tools—and the time of delivery."

He paused, looking away from Kaito.

"I never questioned. I delivered what they asked, always by the river. Sometimes they came to take it themselves. Sometimes... like two days ago, when you were staying here... they told me to bring it *across* the river. For the first time."

"They sent a boat?" Kaito asked.

Bruno nodded slowly.

"Yes. A black wooden boat. No markings. They arranged everything. I crossed over... and what I saw..."

His voice trembled slightly.

"There were lights—so many lights glowing in the trees. Dogs moving silently. Shadows everywhere. I couldn't see faces, but I could feel their power. Something's going on, Kaito. Something bigger than we can imagine."

"Do you think... they're the Bone Eaters?" Kaito whispered.

Bruno didn't answer immediately.

"I don't know. But whoever they are... they're preparing for something. And it's not good."

They agreed to rest for the night. As they parted ways, Kaito whispered:

"We'll talk tomorrow. Don't say anything to Luna. Please."

Bruno nodded. "Okay. Good night, Kaito."

Next Morning

"Kaito! Come fast!" Bruno's voice was urgent.

Kaito rushed outside. "What happened?"

Bruno pulled him aside and showed him a folded note. His voice shook as he spoke.

"Another message. They want **medical kits** and **knives** today. They said they'll leave a boat near the river again."

Kaito took the note and read it silently.

"Did anyone come to give you this?" he asked.

"No one," Bruno replied. 'As always, I found it on the garden grass. I'll take the supplies myself."

"Was the boat big?" Kaito asked.

"Yes. This time it was huge. But maybe because they expected more things…"

Kaito's eyes lit up with a sudden plan.

"Then I'm coming too."

"No, Kaito!" Bruno stopped him. "It's too dangerous. If they see you, they'll kill you… and if anything happens to you, my family could also be at risk."

Kaito looked at Bruno seriously.

"You work in the Wisdom Pack, right? Then tell me—where's the wisdom in staying silent while the darkness grows?"

Bruno looked down, conflicted.

"I promise I won't involve your family. But you have to help me. Please, Bruno. We need to protect all the packs. We can't stay afraid forever.'

There was silence. Then Bruno slowly nodded.

"Alright. But what's the plan?"

Kaito whispered his idea.

"You'll take the supplies on the boat like usual. I'll hide inside—somewhere they won't notice. When we get close to their place, I'll jump into the river quietly and swim to their side. You just return back like nothing happened. Be with your family. Don't wait for me."

Bruno's eyes widened. "Kaito... they will kill you if they catch you."

Kaito smiled, softly.

"It's okay. If I die... I'll die for the packs. Someone has to risk it. Let it be me."

4

The Rise of the Bone Eaters

<hr>

That Night...

The moonlight shimmered gently over the silent trees as Bruno and Kaito quietly stepped out of the house. Luna stood at the door, smiling softly, unaware of the real danger behind this journey. They gave her a casual wave, pretending it was just another night delivery. Neither of them said a word about what was coming.

They rode through the quiet, misty forest trails toward the river, the soft crunch of dried leaves beneath the wheels being the only sound in the dark. When they reached the riverbank, a wooden boat was already waiting — just like the masked dogs had promised.

Bruno parked the vehicle slowly, switched off the lights, and looked around. The air was thick with tension. Together, they lifted the delivery items — a crate filled with medical kits, knives, packed food, and cloths — and carefully loaded them onto the boat.

Kaito looked at Bruno one last time. Bruno's eyes were filled with worry.

Bruno whispered, "Kaito, this is it. Are you sure?"

Kaito nodded with a faint smile. "It's time. I'll be careful. Thank you, Bruno... for trusting me."

Without hesitation, Kaito climbed into the boat and hid under one of the covered crates. The boat began drifting slowly as the river pulled it forward. Nearing the darkened end of the river, where the enemy territory began, Bruno softly tapped on the crate and whispered:

"Take care, my friend. Come back alive."

Kaito whispered back, "Don't worry. I've come this far... I'll finish it."

As the boat got close, Kaito quietly slipped out and dove into the river, disappearing beneath the cold, black water. Bruno stayed on the boat, reached the end, and handed over the crate to the masked dogs waiting silently near the shadows of the forest edge.

Not a single word was spoken. The dogs took the items and vanished into the trees.

Bruno turned the empty boat around, his heart pounding. He looked back once, hoping Kaito had made it safely. Then he rode home, his mind restless, praying Kaito would return.

Kaito Enters the Shadows...

Kaito stepped deeper into the dark forest, guided only by the dim light of his lamp and the echo of his own heartbeat. The trees stood tall and twisted like ancient guards. The air turned colder, heavier. Suddenly, in the distance, he noticed shadows shifting—massive dog-like figures moving silently near a tunnel entrance hidden behind thick roots and stone.

He ducked behind a fallen tree trunk, trying to stay hidden. But his scent must've travelled—two massive dogs sniffed the air and growled low.

Tosa Inu and Dogo Argentino. Towering. Muscular. Eyes glowing faintly in the dark.

Kaito knew it was too late. He turned to run, but before he could move, a **Bully Kutta** leapt in front of him. Behind him, a Cane Corso blocked his escape.

They surrounded him.

Within seconds, he was pinned to the ground, snarling and barking, trying to fight them off—but there were too many.

One of them growled, "Take him inside."

They dragged him toward the tunnel—a wide, rocky opening with ancient carvings scratched into the stone. Flames in hanging torches lit the passage inside, casting long, flickering shadows on the walls.

The air changed as they entered—colder, damper, filled with the scent of blood and iron. The tunnel was long, winding, and guarded. Bones were scattered in the corners. Faint growls and metal clanks echoed throughout.

At the end of the tunnel, the space opened up into a massive underground kingdom.

Stone buildings carved into rock walls. Metal cages holding snarling dogs. Brutal-looking warriors patrolled the paths— Bulldog, Alabais, Presa Canarios, Sarplaninacs—each one stronger and more terrifying than the next.

Kaito's eyes widened. "What is this place…"

One Presa Canario barked, "Welcome to the underworld, traitor."

They dragged him to a corner, tied him with thick chains to an iron pillar, and left him in the dark.

The next morning…

The heavy iron doors creaked open. Kaito, tired but defiant, raised his head.

Footsteps. Heavy. Calculated.

A massive Sarplaninac, scarred and wild-eyed, entered. Behind him walked others, clearing the path.

Kaito growled, barked loudly, struggling in chains. "I'll kill you! You're the ones spoiling the packs! I'll burn this place down myself!"

The guards laughed. None responded.

Suddenly—

ROARRRRRRRRRRRRRRRRRRRRRR!!

A sound unlike anything he had heard.

Everything stopped.

Even the birds in the forest above went silent. The walls shook.

Kaito stopped barking, stunned.

From the shadows walked a beast. Taller than any dog. Coated in black with red eyes. The one they called... **The Bone King**. His name was **Nero** (an Alabai).

He stared down at Kaito.

His voice was calm, but it hit like thunder:

"Remove his chains."

The guards looked shocked.

"But—"

"I said... remove it."

One by one, the iron cuffs around Kaito's legs were unlocked. The clanking echoed in the tunnel.

"Sit, Kaito."

Kaito looked up.

"I prefer standing."

Nero gave a cold smile.

"As you wish."

He turned and walked toward a raised stone that looked like a throne carved by time itself.

As the flames flickered across the walls of the tunnel, he began:

The True Story of the Bone Eaters

ᗡᗡᗡ

The Fall of the Dread Fangs

Long ago, there were six mighty packs spread across the wild lands.

Each had their own rule, their own laws, and unique strengths.

But above them all... stood us — **The Dread Fang Pack.**

They called us *Bone Eaters*.

Not because we were monsters... but because they feared us. We were warriors, protectors, and rulers of the **Kingdom of Fangs** — a united land where no dog starved, and no pack suffered the curse of war.

Every pack had:

· Its own territory.
· Its own laws.
· Its own right to breed, live, and lead.

We held monthly gatherings — led by our noble king, **Varkor**, a mighty Boerboel with unmatched wisdom and strength.

A Mistake at the Border

One day, in a small border pack named **Blood Fang**, which shared land with ours... a young fighter crossed into our territory during training.

He clashed with one of our warriors and wounded him badly.

We punished him — harshly.
Tied him under the blazing sun for three days.

Stripped him of his medal of rank.

But we did **not** take his life.

Nero paused.

His voice trembled — not with anger, but something deeper.

"That's when everything changed," he said.

"Because what we didn't know...

was that pup was the son of Blood Fang's Beta."

Brutu — The Seed of Hate

Name: Brutu

Breed: Pit Bull

Position: Beta of Blood Fang

Brutu was a cold, dangerous figure. Ambitious to the bone.

And when his son returned home — broken, humiliated — Brutu's eyes turned black with hate.

He whispered lies into King Kraven's ears:

"The Dread Fangs are becoming tyrants."

"They punish without trial. They're growing bolder. We're next."

At first, **King Kraven**, a proud but fair old Rottweiler, didn't believe him.

But then... Brutu was found bleeding near the border.

His leg torn. His son... murdered.

We didn't do it.

But the blame was placed.

And from that moment — everything burned.

The Dark Rise of Rumours

One by one, dogs from various packs began to die — in the same brutal fashion:

- Throats torn
- Bones shattered

- Meat missing

And the whispers began:
"The Bone Eaters are hunting again."
We were the heart of the land. Every law, every gathering, every message passed through us.
But suddenly... no one listened.

The Great Betrayal War
It wasn't King Kraven.
It wasn't even Brutu.
Behind the shadows... was a darker mind.
A *black sheep* hiding deep inside Blood Fang.
This dog framed us. Lied about us.
And when the fires of war began... diplomacy was too late.

King Varkor, still unaware of the traitor's existence, sent messages wrapped in blood-red cloth — the symbol of peace.
But no one believed them anymore.
Birds flew across the skies carrying scrolls marked with Varkor's royal paw print — once a symbol of unity, now ignored.

The Packs That Choose War
One by one, every major pack turned against us:

1. **Blood Fang Pack**

   - *Ruler:* King Kraven (Rottweiler)
   - *Believed Dread Fang murdered their own.*

2. **Sky Watchers**

   - *Ruler:* Zyra (Siberian Husky, visionary)
   - *Silent, but sided with Blood Fang out of fear.*

3. **Pack of Valor**

   - *Ruler:* Baros (German Shepherd)
   - *Believed in honour — believed the lies.*

4. **Wisdom Pack**

   - *Ruler:* Mira (Golden Retriever)

   - *Strategists. Neutral, but pushed into war by false evidence.*

6. **Trade Pack**

   - *Ruler:* Juzo (Beagle)
   - *Controlled food and medicine. Their loyalty was bought by Blood Fang.*

The First Strike
The war didn't begin with barks — it began with silence.
Dread Fang patrols went missing.
Their border guards were attacked in the night.
Then... the sky turned black with smoke.
The first attack came from Blood Fang, ambushing the outer villages of the Dread Fang lands.
Old dogs, pups, and young females were dragged away and killed.
And when Dread Fang responded —
They were labeled as savages.
The Real War Begins
The Dread Fangs were outnumbered... but they were fierce.

Their warriors were trained in jungle combat, tunnel Défense, and river ambushes.

Fields burned.

Rivers ran red.

The air was filled with howls, growls, and death.

The Battle of Blackroot Pass lasted 3 days.

- The Sky Watchers attacked from above the cliffside, dropping boulders.
- Pack of Valor stormed the tunnels with hounds like Mudhol, Rajapalayam, and Kombai.
- The Trade Pack cut off food supplies.

Still, the Dread Fangs held the line.

Betrayal Within Hope

Some dogs — kind-hearted ones — refused the lies.

- From Sky Watchers, a **husky** named **Yuro** helped female Dread Fangs escape through river tunnels.
- From Valor, an **Indian Pariah** named **Leo** hid pups in her pack's nursery.
- From Wisdom, a young **Shih Tzu** called **Remin** forged fake death scrolls to smuggle survivors.

Because of these few brave souls, some lives were saved. But not enough.

The Death of King Varkor

On the final day, Blood Fang and Pack of Valor surrounded the Fang Fortress, the heart of Dread Fang lands.

King **Varkor** stood atop the main gate, wounded but unbent.

His last command?

"Protect the pups. Save the mothers.
Let the fire eat me, not my people."
He faced King karven himself in a duel.
The ground shook.
The sky cried.
And when the dust cleared...
Varkor was no more.

The Fall of Dread Fang
After Varkor death, the enemies swarmed the fortress.
They broke down dens.
Burned sacred stones.
And gave the Dread Fangs a new name in blood:
"Bone Eaters."
A name meant to erase honour.
To turn truth into horror.
But the Dread Fangs who escaped...
They remember.
And one day...
We will return.

5

The Truth Unveiled

We ran deep into a hidden forest — untouched by the paws of any pack.

It was dark. Silent. Protected by nature itself.

We called it **The Forest of Shadows.**

No pack dared to enter.

And we liked it that way.

There, in the heart of the shadows, we chose a king — **Ragnar**, the last son of the true Dread Fang king.

A mighty **Boerboel** with unmatched strength and the wisdom of our fallen ancestors

But Ragnar did not rule us as a warlord.

He ruled as a protector.

He taught us to defend, not destroy.

He carved the truth into every pup's paw — our mark, our identity.

Ragnar married a noble **Rhodesian Ridgeback** named **Breeze.**

And then... on one stormy night, Ragnar became a father.

Breeze gave birth to a pup with fire in his blood... and the sacred mark of Dread Fang glowing on his paw.

Ragnar named him **Rexor** — *"Fire from Ashes."*

Nero paused.

His voice softened, as if he had lived every moment himself.

"Rexor was... different.

Smart. Strong.

But most of all — curious.

He'd always ask Ragnar,

'Why do we hide?'

'Why do the other packs hate us?'

But Ragnar never answered.

Still, Rexor grew fast — faster than any pup before him. And silently... he began to slip out of the forest.

He wanted to see the world with his own eyes.

And during one of those secret visits...

He saw her."

Nero's tone turned almost... tender.

"She was from the Sky Watcher pack.

A beautiful dog.

Soft-coated, gentle, with a golden stripe running down her back like the sun kissing the horizon at dawn.

Her name was **Yuki**—an **Akita**.

She lived near the edge of the riverside village...

Graceful, quiet, curious.

She had eyes like the calm before a storm — soft, deep, and knowing.

She had come to study in the Wisdom Pack... to learn the old ways.

Their first meeting was under the full moon, near the River Morrow.

It started with glances.

Then words.

Then... stars witnessed what no one else could.

Every night, they met —
beneath the skies, beyond the rules,
where only silence and moonlight knew their names.
Rexor didn't tell anyone.
He knew what it meant...
A Bone Eater falling in love with an outsider?
Unforgivable.
But love...
Love doesn't follow rules.
It doesn't bow to bloodlines or ancient grudges.
Days passed.
Seasons shifted.
And then... one night...
Yuki told him—she was pregnant."
Kaito's ears twitched.
His breathing changed — Nero noticed... but didn't stop.
"Rexor was overjoyed.
A new life. A secret future.
But around the same time... Ragnar fell ill.
And the weight of the pack dropped onto Rexor's shoulders overnight. He was trying to lead and protect... and he couldn't see Yuki for many days.
And when he finally went to find her...
It was too late."
Nero's voice hardened.
His claws scraped lightly against the stone floor.
"She was hiding.
The other packs had found out.
They said she carried the blood of a Bone Eater.
You see...
None of them believed the Bone Eaters still existed.
The name had become myth.
A warning. A ghost.

But a pup born of their blood?

They wanted her dead.

She ran.

In the middle of the night,
she reached the River Morrow.
Alone. Trembling.
She gave birth beneath the pale moonlight...

Three pups.

Rexor arrived just in time to hold one of them. A strong male pup. He dipped the pup in the river to clean him... but behind him—they came.

They took her. They took the other two pups. Rexor saw them only for a second before Yuki looked at him, tears in her eyes, and signed him with one last glance...

'Save at least one.'

He marked that pup. A burned symbol on his paw, something only our pack knows. Something only a Bone Eater would recognize."

Nero's eyes locked with Kaito's.

"Rexor hid the pup in a food truck leaving near the river. Then he turned... and fought.

He didn't survive.

That pup was carried away... into the unknown. And all these years... we searched. We waited. We wondered if he lived."

He walked up to Kaito and raised his paw slowly.

"But then I saw you barking. The rage, the fire, the way you stood. And when I saw your paw..."

He touched Kaito's leg gently, revealing the faint symbol burned on his skin.

"It was you.

You are Rexor's son.

The last flame of the Bone Eaters.

The heir to the Dread Fang."

Kaito's Awakening: From Lost to Legacy

The tunnel echoed with silence as Nero's words faded into the cold air.

Kaito stood frozen, eyes wide, heart pounding. His legs trembled, not from fear—but from the weight of the truth.

He wasn't just a stray.

He wasn't a nameless mutt surviving on scraps.

He was Rexor son.

A prince born in shadows.

A spark from a fallen kingdom.

His throat tightened, and for the first time, Kaito whispered,

"So... they were my parents?"

Nero nodded slowly.

"Yes. Kaito—the fire-hearted son of Rexor, and Yuki—the star that never feared the dark. You carry both their blood. You carry their pain... and their purpose."

Tears threatened to fall, but Kaito blinked them away. He was sad—sad for what was lost. For a mother he never knew. For a father who died protecting him.

And yet... he felt something bloom in his chest.

Pride.

"All this time... I thought I was nothing," Kaito said softly. "But I'm not just anyone. I'm a Bone Eater."

Nero nodded again. "And not just any Bone Eater. You are our last light."

But Kaito wasn't done. His voice turned sharp with hunger for truth.

"Tell me, Nero. Who did this? Who destroyed our kingdom? Who spreads these lies?"

Nero's face darkened.

"That... is the question we still don't fully know."

He began walking, slow steps echoing in the silence.

"We know the enemy came from Blood Fang. Someone with power. Someone who wanted Dread Fang broken forever."

"We never killed their king. We never touched their lands. But they blamed us. They called us bone eaters, monsters. The real war was started with a rumour—a lie meant to make all packs rise against us."

"Do you remember the Husky from Skywatchers? The one who found out the truth?"

Kaito's eyes narrowed. "Yeah... the one they said we killed."

Nero's tone grew colder.

"He was investigating. He found the trail—the truth. He knew we weren't the monsters. He was on his way to tell the Blood Fang King the truth. But before it could spread beyond, both were found dead. And outside those walls, the lie lived on.

"Kaito's heart twisted.

"And once again, they blamed us."

Nero looked him dead in the eye.

"Same lies. Same trap. And we realized... someone out there still wants the Bone Eaters gone. Not just forgotten—erased."

The fire in Kaito's chest exploded.

He stood up, chest heaving, his body glowing with that inner strength that could no longer hide.

He wasn't just some angry fighter now.

He was a leader.

"Then we won't run anymore," he said firmly.

"We'll find the truth. We'll clear our name. And if they want a war... we'll give them a reason to fear the name Bone Eater again."

All the dogs in the tunnel looked at him—not as a prisoner—but as a king rising from ash.

6
The War of the Kingdom

The Message from Blood Fang

For the first time in years, a bird flew into the heart of the forest—a royal owl and trained only by the Blood Fang.

The Bone Eaters stared in shock.

Nero slowly unrolled the scroll tied to its leg.

The ancient seal of Blood Fang cracked open—and beneath it, were words written in sharp, clawed strokes:

"We want peace. But also, truth. One dog from your side. One from ours. Meet us at the border of the Dead Hollow Forest.

There... we will tell you who your real enemy is."

The silence in the den was thick—until Cane Carso, the most aggressive fighter among them, growled with rage.

"A trap! We waited all these years and now they dare play games?"

His eyes burned with fury as he stood up and faced everyone.

"They destroyed our pack. Killed our king. Lied to every kingdom. And now they want to talk?

No. I say we burn them all. If they call us Bone Eaters—fine. Let's show them why."

The crowd murmured in agreement—rage clouding judgment.

But before it could boil over, Kaito stepped forward.

His voice wasn't loud—but it was firm. Like steel beneath silk.

"No."

Everyone turned toward him.

"We are not Bone Eaters. They gave us that name. We are Dread Fang. Sons and daughters of kings and warriors. We don't kill without truth."

Cane Carso bared his teeth.

"They are part of the reason we fell, Kaito. Why should we believe their message?"

Kaito stepped closer.

"Because we've been in hiding for too long. Living in the dark like we're guilty.

What if the real enemy is still out there? Watching us fight each other like fools?"

He held up the scroll.

"This letter... it may be a trap. But it could also be the first crack in the wall they built around us."

The place fell quiet. Every dog stared, hearts torn between revenge and reason.

Kaito's voice dropped low, almost a whisper.

"If we start a war now, we prove everyone right. But if we find the truth...

We win more than a battle.

We win our name back."

Nero watched the young dog with proud eyes.

For the first time... they weren't following a fighter.

They were following a leader.

The Night Journey: Truth Under the Moonlight

The forest was silent.

Only the moonlight touched the ground as Kaito prepared to leave. He tightened the cloth on his leg — the same cloth with the Dread Fang paw symbol his father once wore.

Nero stood in front of him, firm and unmoving.

"You are the King now, Kaito. I won't let you go. This meeting could be a trap."

Kaito placed his paw gently on Nero's shoulder.

"I know, old friend. But this is our only chance. We waited too long.

I'll go. Alone. Like they asked."

The pack behind them began to grow restless. Nero's eyes searched for an answer.

"Then... at least let Presa Canario go with you. He'll stay in the shadows. Won't speak.

Just in case."

Kaito gave a slight nod.

"Fine. But he won't step in. This is between me and them."

Kaito arrived at the edge of the Dead Hollow Forest. A faint fog hugged the soil. The scent of pine and betrayal filled the air.

Waiting there, calmly and sharply, stood a tall Doberman — muscular, lean, with scars under his eyes and a black collar with the Blood Fang mark.

"So, you came," the **Zoran** (Doberman) said, with a hollow smile.

Kaito stood still.

"You asked for truth. I'm here.

But I don't see your King.

Just a bodyguard pretending to be brave."

Zoran chuckled.

"Still the sharp tongue, like your father.

The Bone Eaters were never weak.
But your time is over."

Kaito didn't flinch.

"We're not Bone Eaters. That name was given to us in hate.

We are Dread Fang."

"Dread Fang? That name was buried long ago."

Zoran looked around the trees, cautious.

"You ask about the King? Let me tell you something...
The Blood Fang King was a puppet."

Kaito narrowed his eyes.

"What do you mean?"

The Zoran lowered his voice.

"In Blood Fang... the real rulers are a secret lineage of Kangal dogs.

Their blood runs deep in our pack's history.

Every decision, every battle, every betrayal — they controlled it all."

Kaito took a step forward.

"So.... the King was just a face?"

"Yes. A name to show the world. But the Kangal family? They ruled from the shadows."

Kaito's heart began to race.

"Then what about the meeting? The one between your King, the Kangal, and the Husky?
What happened?"

Zoran 's eyes darkened.

"It all started one night. I was on guard duty at the Blood Fang fortress.

Suddenly, the Husky, one of the King's most trusted messengers, arrived —

But something was wrong. His fur was dusty, eyes full of fear and urgency.

He didn't bark.
He whispered."

"I didn't waste time. I ran to the Kangal first — the real ruler behind our King.
Not many know this, Kaito, but in Blood Fang, the Kangal family makes all the rules.
The King is just a face for the outside world."

Kaito's eyes widened.

"So, the King wasn't really in control?"

"No. The Kangal gave orders from the shadows.
But this night... even he was shaken."

"The Kangal said, *'Bring the King immediately. But keep this quiet. Not a soul should know.'*
I followed. And within minutes, all three were in a secret chamber.
I wasn't supposed to listen, Kaito...
But I hid behind the roots. I had to know."

Zoran's voice dropped lower.

"That night... changed everything."

"The Husky turned to both the King and the Kangal, and said:
'We made a mistake. The Bone Eaters... they are not our enemy.
The real enemy is in our own pack.
Someone powerful. Someone hiding. And they're the one who started the war.'

Kaito's jaw tightened.

"He knew we were alive?"

"Yes. He said it himself — ***'The Bone Eaters are alive. Scattered. But not broken.'***
He wanted to make things right."

Zoran looked away for a moment.

"The King stood silent.
Then he said: **'We've done something unforgivable...
But I'll find the real traitor.
Even if it means giving my life.'**
Kaito's heart pounded.
"And the Kangal?"
"He agreed.
He said: *'You both will go meet the Bone Eaters yourselves.
Ask for forgiveness.
And we will find the one who betrayed us from inside.'*"

The Secret Departure

"The King and the Husky left that night — quietly.
Only I and the Kangal knew.
The Kangal ordered me:
*'Watch over the kingdom for two days.
Tell no one. Not even the generals.'*"
Kaito's voice cracked.
"And then?"
Zoran's face grew cold.
"Then... everything fell apart."
The flames of the campfire crackled, but Kaito didn't feel their warmth.

Zoran's voice turned hollow, full of scars and silence as he continued his story.

"You think it ended with that secret meeting, Kaito?
No... the real nightmare began that same night."

The Enemy Within

"After the King and Husky left for the forest...
The Kangal called a meeting with his trusted dogs."
"I hid in the shadows again.
I thought maybe he would protect them.
But what I heard made my blood freeze."
Zoran's eyes glowed with pain.

"He said... 'They are fools. The moment they show mercy to the Bone Eaters, our rule ends.
We will no longer be gods — just names in history.
I will not let that happen.'"

"That moment, I knew... the Kangal family was behind everything.
The war. The lies. The rumours. All of it."

"That night, I followed the Kangal. He took his elite killers — not many, just enough.
Silent. Deadly.
They followed the King and Husky deep into the woods...
Like shadows."

"The King and Husky didn't know.
They were ready to meet the Bone Eaters.
They were full of hope."

Zoran paused, holding back a growl.

"Then it happened —
In the darkest part of the woods, they attacked."

"The Husky fought hard.
The King roared.
But they were outnumbered."

"Just before the King fell... I heard him say...
'We only wanted peace...'"

"The Kangal walked up to him and whispered:
'Peace is for the weak. Ruling is for the strong.
And I will rule. Forever.'"

The Return of Lies

"After that... he returned to the kingdom.
Calm. Bloody. But smiling."

"He told everyone that the Bone Eaters had killed the King and Husky.
He said they betrayed us again.
And... they believed him."

Kaito's heart shattered. His claws dug into the soil.

"Why didn't you tell anyone?!" he asked.

Zoran lowered his head.

"I tried.

But I'm not leader, Kaito.

Just a low-ranked guard.

They would've killed me too."

He looked up slowly.

"They killed the King... What am I in front of them? Nothing. I was waiting for the right leader. They know... they know that somewhere, Dread Fang blood still lives. That's why I sent the birds. Hoping—praying—you'd find the truth."

Kaito stood still. His body trembled — not with fear, but fire.

"They lied to us all this time.."

"They killed my parents... to rule with fear."

"No more."

His eyes met the Zoran's.

"You did right. Even if no one listened."

"Now, I will."

The flames behind them rose, as if the spirits of the fallen were waking.

The moonlight fell like silver on the Zoran's face as he leaned in closer to Kaito.

"You asked me... why the Kangals did all this?"

"Why they betrayed the King, the Husky... and framed your family?"

"Let me tell you, Kaito — this hatred is older than you, older than me...

It started three generations ago."

The Past That Bled – Kangal vs Bone Eater

"Long ago, before your father became King, the Kangal family ruled a small pack under the Dread Fang reign," Zoran began. "They were powerful. Feared. Cruel. But they wanted more—they wanted everything."

"The Dread Fang—your ancestors—refused to let fear govern the packs. So, they united everyone and defeated the Kangal's in war. That war turned a small pack into a great kingdom."

"But your great-grandfather didn't kill them. He showed mercy. Gave them land. Safety. A chance to start again."

He shook his head.

"But mercy... mercy was something the Kangal's never understood."

"From that day, the Kangal line swore an oath:
**'We may lose power... but one day we'll take it back.
Not with strength. But with lies.'"**

"They waited in silence. They married into noble bloodlines in the Blood Fang pack. They whispered in ears. Poisoned minds."

"They spread lies that the Bone Eaters were planning a coup.
They leaked false letters, trained spies...
and made your kind look like monsters."

"And when war broke out, they didn't fight.
They watched —
while your people were slaughtered."

"After the war, when your Great-grandfather found out the truth, he decided to make peace...
But it was too late."

The Kangal betrayed him.

"They killed him and crowned the King's son—a boy who still doesn't know that his throne was built on blood."

He looked away, disgusted.

"Kangal doesn't wear a crown. But he holds the strings. If he had taken the crown, everyone would've suspected. But like a snake in the dark, he rules from the shadows."

"The King obeys him. Trusts him. Loves him like an uncle."

"But make no mistake, Kaito...

Kangal is the true ruler.

And he won't stop... until the last Bone Eater breathes no more."

Kaito's ears lowered. His eyes burned with anger and heartbreak.

"So, this was never just about war...

It was about revenge."

"My Great-grandfather showed them mercy.

And they answered with betrayal."

"They made the world believe we were monsters...

Just to rewrite history."

He turned to the Zoran.

"Not anymore.

The truth will rise.

And this time — they'll face justice."

Kaito was right. There was something in his eyes—an emotion too raw to ignore, a truth clawing its way to the surface.

"We have to save all the packs before it's too late," he said, his voice trembling with urgency.

Beside him stood the fierce and loyal Zoran.

Just as Zoran opened his mouth to respond, a deafening sound tore through the sky.

"DONG... DONG..."—a slow, heavy bell rang out, each toll dragging like a weight of doom.

A thunderous echo rolled across the kingdom like an avalanche.

Zoran's ears twitched. His face turned rigid.

"It's too late, Kaito..." he murmured, his voice low and grim. "That sound... it's the war bell."

The air grew still for a moment, like the calm before a deadly storm.

"No," Kaito said, his heart pounding. "We have to stop it before it starts. No one should die. Not a single dog. This war... it can't happen."

Zoran's gaze dropped to the ground. "Kaito... things changed when you were in the forest. You don't know what's been happening out here. The kingdom is in chaos. The news channels—every single one—spread fake stories."

"What kind of stories?" Kaito asked, his voice growing sharp.

"That the Bone Eaters are back. That they've returned to destroy us all. Every pack heard it. And the Council... they met, decided the Bone Eaters were a threat that needed to be erased completely."

Kaito's eyes widened.

"It was never about truth," Zoran continued, his voice laced with bitterness. "It was a trap. A grand plan, forged by the Kangal family. They're playing everyone like pawns. There's no time to figure it out. We have to stop the packs from turning on each other."

"I'll start with mine," Kaito said, determination blazing in his chest. "Even if my legs give out, I'll run."

And he did.

With his heart pounding and his legs aching, Kaito bolted through the dense forest. Branches whipped at his face, blood trickled from his scraped paws, but he didn't stop. He couldn't.

Every thud of his paw against the earth was a drumbeat of urgency.

Presa Canario, silent as ever, ran beside him.

No words.

No questions.

Just breath. And fear.

When they finally reached the edge of the territory, they froze.

Something was wrong.

The Bone Eater dens were... empty.

No guards. No scents. No fires.

Only the wind and the cold silence that wrapped around them like a shroud.

"Where are they...?" Kaito gasped, panting.

"Where is everyone?"

Presa sniffed the air, every muscle in her body tensed. he turned to him, eyes wide.

"They're gone."

The forest around them seemed to exhale all at once.

Kaito's heart dropped.

"The war..." Presa said softly. "It's already begun."

And then, in the far distance—low and chilling—the war bell rang again.

Its sound rolled through the valleys, over the rivers, and across the skies.

The kingdom of Fangs had entered the Valley of Roars.

And the war had truly begun.

The Valley of Roars – The War Begins

The skies above the *Valley of Roars* churned with dark clouds. A storm brewed—not of nature, but of fury, vengeance, and centuries of mistrust.

From every corner of the kingdom, they came.

Over **300 distinct breeds**—majestic, fierce, loyal.

Over **a thousand mixed-breed warriors**—strong, untamed, proud.

Each pack stood under their own banners:

Blood Fang, scarred by generations of battle.

Trade Pack, built on loyalty and alliance.

Wisdom Pack, aged with truth but wounded by propaganda.

Sky Watchers, silent guardians of the north winds.

And **Pack Valor**, heart of the land.

But their hearts beat the same beat—one that craved revenge.

Against one enemy: *The Bone Eaters.*

They had been labeled monsters. But were they?

Kaito and Presa Canario reached the top of the valley hill, panting, bloodied from the wild forest. Behind them, Zoran, the stoic Doberman, appeared like a shadow of war—silent, powerful, and watching everything unfold.

Zoran stared at the armies gathering below. "It's done, Kaito," he said, his voice low and heavy. "We can't stop this. It's too big now. Too dangerous. The Kings of every pack are here. The Councils too. This is the end of the Bone Eaters."

Below them, the field rumbled with growls, war chants, and the sound of claws against stone. The earth shook with thousands of paws.

Kaito stood still on the hilltop, heart thundering.

This can't be the end... Not like this.

"I can't breathe," he whispered. "Their roars... they want to be heard. But in this crowd, no truth will echo. Only blood."

And blood did flow.

The war began with a roar louder than the thunder above.

Steel-like teeth clashed.

Fur flew.

Cries of pain rang across the valley like a broken song.

It was chaos.

It was madness.

It was... wrong.

Then—

BOOOOOM! – Drawn out and powerful.

The storm answered.

A blinding wind swept through the valley.

Lightning cracked across the sky like the cry of an ancient god.

And suddenly—

Silence.

Everything... stopped.

The storm wasn't just weather—it was a sign. A pause. A breath from the universe itself.

Zoran and Presa looked at each other. Then, without a word, they rolled a **massive boulder** down the hill, sending it crashing onto the war field, drawing every eye.

Then—Kaito stepped forward.

His voice rose—shaky at first, then strong, like the heart of a pack leader reborn.

"This isn't war. This is **slaughter**. You were told the Bone Eaters are your enemies. But who told you that? Who *benefits* from your anger?"

Murmurs rippled through the crowd.

One warrior from the Blood Fang pack growled, "You have Bone Eater blood too, don't you?"

Gasps followed. Kaito didn't flinch.

"Yes. I do. And that blood? It's not evil. It's **truth**. But if you don't trust me... trust **your own**. Doberman Zoran—his family served this kingdom for decades. Listen to *him*."

Zoran stepped forward. Eyes everywhere locked on him. The fearless, undefeated warrior of the Blood Fang Pack.

"Kaito speaks the truth," Zoran declared. "The real enemy... is the **Kangal family**. They spread the lies. They poisoned your hearts. And for what? *Power. Control. Fear.*"

Another voice called out, "Where's the proof?!"

Kaito reached into a pouch tied to his side and held up a **letter—sealed with the royal bone crest.** The final message from King Kale.

"The late King Kael left this behind," he said, "but they hid it. Suppressed it. This is his truth—not mine. *'Bone Eaters are not our enemies. The stories are false. I plan to go to their den, to seek peace and forgiveness.'*"

Zoran held up a **paw print**, inked in red.

"This... is the mark of peace. Given by a Husky who stood with Bone Eaters till the end."

The valley stood still.

Eyes darted toward the Kangal family, once noble, now trembling under thousands of stares.

And then—

A low growl.

From the back of the Bone Eater formation, a **Bulldog**, face scarred with years of torment, walked slowly forward. His eyes—red with tears, not rage.

He didn't speak.

He didn't need to.

He lunged.

The first blow fell.

Not on a Bone Eater.

But on the *Kangal patriarch*.

And in seconds—

Every lie crumbled.

Every warrior, from every pack, turned toward the Kangal bloodline.

The hunters... became the hunted.

Within minutes, the legacy of the Kangal family fell.

Every root pulled.

Every mask broken.

For the first time in years,

truth roared louder than war.

And from the hill, Kaito watched... not with pride.

But with tears.

The war they feared had become a war for *truth*.

The **Valley of Roars** was no longer a battlefield.

It was the birthplace of a new era.

The War Ends – Rise of Peace

The war that thundered through the *Valley of Roars* had finally come to an end.

But not with more blood.

7
The Final Howl

The storm above cleared. The clouds parted, as if the skies themselves had been holding their breath. Light poured onto the valley floor where warriors from all packs stood still, breathing the air of *a new dawn*.

For the first time in decades, the name **Bone Eaters** was no longer whispered in hatred.
The truth had set them free.

An official bark echoed across the land, heard by every dog—from the forest dens to the northern cliffs:

"Let it be known, by all Packs and Kingdoms, the name *Bone Eaters* shall be erased from shame. They are no longer cursed. They are part of us—our blood, our breath, our kin."

Cheers followed. Howls filled the air. Some barked. Some cried. But all felt **lighter**, like a curse had been lifted.

Among the celebrations, one declaration changed history.

The *council of packs* stood together in the centre of the valley and made it official:

"The **Dread Fang Pack**, once hidden in darkness, now stands in light. As of this day, they are the **Pack of Rulers**—guardians of peace and justice in the **Kingdom of**

Fangs."

The moment had come.

All turned to the hilltop where **Kaito** stood, battle-worn, but glowing with purpose.

Nore, the leader of the Dread Fangs, stepped forward and lowered his head.

"The crown is yours, Kaito. You freed us. You led with courage, not claws."

Silence.

And then—Kaito smiled.

He looked around. So many warriors. So many packs. So many *hopes* placed on his shoulders.

And he said gently:

"No, Nore. I fought... but **you led** us through the darkness. When everyone had given up... *you didn't.* That makes you the king.
And I... I just want peace."

"Tears welled up in Nore's eyes, and he nodded quietly as Kaito gently placed the crown upon his head, the weight of it settling into his heart."

The valley howled in celebration.

Kaito was free.

Return to Trade Pack

Weeks passed.

Kaito returned to the **Trade Pack**, where his old life waited like a warm blanket.

He stepped into the bakery—and there he was.

Muffin, the grumpy-but-golden-hearted pug, barking orders as usual.

Next to him, the ever-hyper, always-loyal **Rolo** saw Kaito.

His eyes widened. His ears perked.

And in the blink of an eye—**he jumped!**

"KAITOOOOO!" Rolo howled, tackling him into a playful wrestle. "YOU'RE ALIVE! I thought you'd die a *hero* and leave me to run this smelly bakery alone!"

Kaito laughed, pushing him back playfully. "Oh please. You'd make a kingdom out of junk and leftover bones."

Rolo sniffled. "Don't joke. I really thought... I was going to be alone. Again."

Kaito's smile softened. He hugged Rolo tightly. "I promised I'd come back. Brothers don't break promises."

Suddenly, Rolo's eyes twinkled. "Alsoooo... GUESS WHAT? Rosie said YES!"

Kaito blinked. "Wait, what?! Rosie? As in the serious dog with no sense of humour?"

"Yeah! Turns out she *does* have a heart under all that bark!" Rolo said proudly, wagging his tail. "But now... we gotta go talk to her dad. You coming?"

Kaito mock gasped. "To face *her father*? The one who chews through fence posts like they're biscuits?"

"Hey! That's a *rumour*! He only did it once!" Rolo grinned.

And just like that—peace felt real.

A Kingdom Rebuilt

The packs continued to rebuild, not just walls and homes—but **trust**.

For the first time, **all packs met under one council**, with King **Nore** on the throne but with Kaito as their *peacekeeper*, storyteller, and advisor.

The **Valley of Roars** wasn't feared anymore.

It became a sacred place.

A place where truth won.

Where unity began.

Where *a roar became a whisper of peace.*